W9-AWI-059

RESURGAM!!!

THIS BOOK BELONGS TO

....

THE TALE
OF
JEMIMA PUDDLE-DUCK

THE TALE OF
JEMIMA PUDDLE-DUCK

BY

BEATRIX POTTER

Author of
"The Tale of Peter Rabbit", &c.

FREDERICK WARNE

*The reproductions in this book have been made using
the most modern electronic scanning methods from entirely
new transparencies of Beatrix Potter's original watercolours.
They enable Beatrix Potter's skill as an artist to be appreciated
as never before, not even during her own lifetime.*

FREDERICK WARNE

Published by the Penguin Group
27 Wrights Lane, London W8 5TZ, England
Penguin Books USA Inc., 375 Hudson Street, New York, New York 10014, USA
Penguin Books Australia Ltd, Ringwood, Victoria, Australia
Penguin Books Canada Ltd, 10 Alcorn Avenue, Toronto, Ontario, Canada M4V 3B2
Penguin Books (NZ) Ltd, 182-190 Wairau Road, Auckland 10, New Zealand

Penguin Books Ltd, Registered Offices: Harmondsworth, Middlesex, England

First published 1908
Published with new reproductions 1987
This paperback edition first published 1991

Printed and bound in Great Britain by
William Clowes Limited, Beccles and London

A FARMYARD TALE

FOR

RALPH AND BETSY

WHAT a funny sight it is to see a brood of ducklings with a hen!
—Listen to the story of Jemima Puddle-duck, who was annoyed because the farmer's wife would not let her hatch her own eggs.

HER sister-in-law, Mrs. Rebeccah Puddle-duck, was perfectly willing to leave the hatching to some one else —"I have not the patience to sit on a nest for twenty-eight days; and no more have you, Jemima. You would let them go cold; you know you would!"

"I wish to hatch my own eggs; I will hatch them all by myself," quacked Jemima Puddle-duck.

SHE tried to hide her eggs; but they were always found and carried off.

Jemima Puddle-duck became quite desperate. She determined to make a nest right away from the farm.

SHE set off on a fine spring afternoon along the cart-road that leads over the hill.

She was wearing a shawl and a poke bonnet.

15

16

WHEN she reached the top of the hill, she saw a wood in the distance.

She thought that it looked a safe quiet spot.

JEMIMA PUDDLE-DUCK was not much in the habit of flying. She ran downhill a few yards flapping her shawl, and then she jumped off into the air.

18

SHE flew beautifully when she had got a good start.

She skimmed along over the tree-tops until she saw an open place in the middle of the wood, where the trees and brushwood had been cleared.

JEMIMA alighted rather heavily, and began to waddle about in search of a convenient dry nesting-place. She rather fancied a tree-stump amongst some tall fox-gloves.

But—seated upon the stump, she was startled to find an elegantly dressed gentleman reading a newspaper.

He had black prick ears and sandy coloured whiskers.

"Quack?" said Jemima Puddle-duck, with her head and her bonnet on one side— "Quack?"

23

24

THE gentleman raised his eyes above his newspaper and looked curiously at Jemima—

"Madam, have you lost your way?" said he. He had a long bushy tail which he was sitting upon, as the stump was somewhat damp.

Jemima thought him mighty civil and handsome. She explained that she had not lost her way, but that she was trying to find a convenient dry nesting-place.

"AH! is that so? indeed!" said the gentleman with sandy whiskers, looking curiously at Jemima. He folded up the newspaper, and put it in his coat-tail pocket.

Jemima complained of the superfluous hen.

"Indeed! how interesting! I wish I could meet with that fowl. I would teach it to mind its own business!"

"BUT as to a nest—there is no difficulty: I have a sackful of feathers in my wood-shed. No, my dear madam, you will be in nobody's way. You may sit there as long as you like," said the bushy long-tailed gentleman.

He led the way to a very retired, dismal-looking house amongst the fox-gloves.

It was built of faggots and turf, and there were two broken pails, one on top of another, by way of a chimney.

"THIS is my summer residence; you would not find my earth—my winter house—so convenient," said the hospitable gentleman.

There was a tumble-down shed at the back of the house, made of old soap-boxes. The gentleman opened the door, and showed Jemima in.

31

THE shed was almost quite full of feathers—it was almost suffocating; but it was comfortable and very soft.

Jemima Puddle-duck was rather surprised to find such a vast quantity of feathers. But it was very comfortable; and she made a nest without any trouble at all.

WHEN she came out, the sandy whiskered gentleman was sitting on a log reading the newspaper—at least he had it spread out, but he was looking over the top of it.

He was so polite, that he seemed almost sorry to let Jemima go home for the night. He promised to take great care of her nest until she came back again next day.

He said he loved eggs and ducklings; he should be proud to see a fine nestful in his wood-shed.

JEMIMA PUDDLE-DUCK came every afternoon; she laid nine eggs in the nest. They were greeny white and very large. The foxy gentleman admired them immensely. He used to turn them over and count them when Jemima was not there.

At last Jemima told him that she intended to begin to sit next day—"and I will bring a bag of corn with me, so that I need never leave my nest until the eggs are hatched. They might catch cold," said the conscientious Jemima.

"MADAM, I beg you not to trouble yourself with a bag; I will provide oats. But before you commence your tedious sitting, I intend to give you a treat. Let us have a dinner-party all to ourselves!

"May I ask you to bring up some herbs from the farm-garden to make a savoury omelette? Sage and thyme, and mint and two onions, and some parsley. I will provide lard for the stuff—lard for the omelette," said the hospitable gentleman with sandy whiskers.

38

JEMIMA PUDDLE-DUCK was a simpleton: not even the mention of sage and onions made her suspicious.

She went round the farm-garden, nibbling off snippets of all the different sorts of herbs that are used for stuffing roast duck.

AND she waddled into the kitchen, and got two onions out of a basket.

The collie-dog Kep met her coming out, "What are you doing with those onions? Where do you go every afternoon by yourself, Jemima Puddle-duck?"

Jemima was rather in awe of the collie; she told him the whole story.

The collie listened, with his wise head on one side; he grinned when she described the polite gentleman with sandy whiskers.

HE asked several questions about the wood, and about the exact position of the house and shed.

Then he went out, and trotted down the village. He went to look for two fox-hound puppies who were out at walk with the butcher.

JEMIMA PUDDLE-DUCK
went up the cart-road for
the last time, on a sunny afternoon. She was rather bur-
dened with bunches of herbs
and two onions in a bag.

She flew over the wood, and
alighted opposite the house of
the bushy long-tailed gentleman.

HE was sitting on a log;
he sniffed the air, and
kept glancing uneasily round
the wood. When Jemima
alighted he quite jumped.

"Come into the house as
soon as you have looked at
your eggs. Give me the herbs
for the omelette. Be sharp!"

He was rather abrupt.
Jemima Puddle-duck had
never heard him speak like
that.

She felt surprised, and un-
comfortable.

WHILE she was inside she heard pattering feet round the back of the shed. Some one with a black nose sniffed at the bottom of the door, and then locked it.

Jemima became much alarmed.

52

A MOMENT afterwards there were most awful noises—barking, baying, growls and howls, squealing and groans.

And nothing more was ever seen of that foxy-whiskered gentleman.

PRESENTLY Kep opened the door of the shed, and let out Jemima Puddle-duck.

Unfortunately the puppies rushed in and gobbled up all the eggs before he could stop them.

He had a bite on his ear and both the puppies were limping.

55

J EMIMA PUDDLE-DUCK
was escorted home in tears
on account of those eggs.

58

SHE laid some more in June, and she was permitted to keep them herself: but only four of them hatched.

Jemima Puddle-duck said that it was because of her nerves; but she had always been a bad sitter.